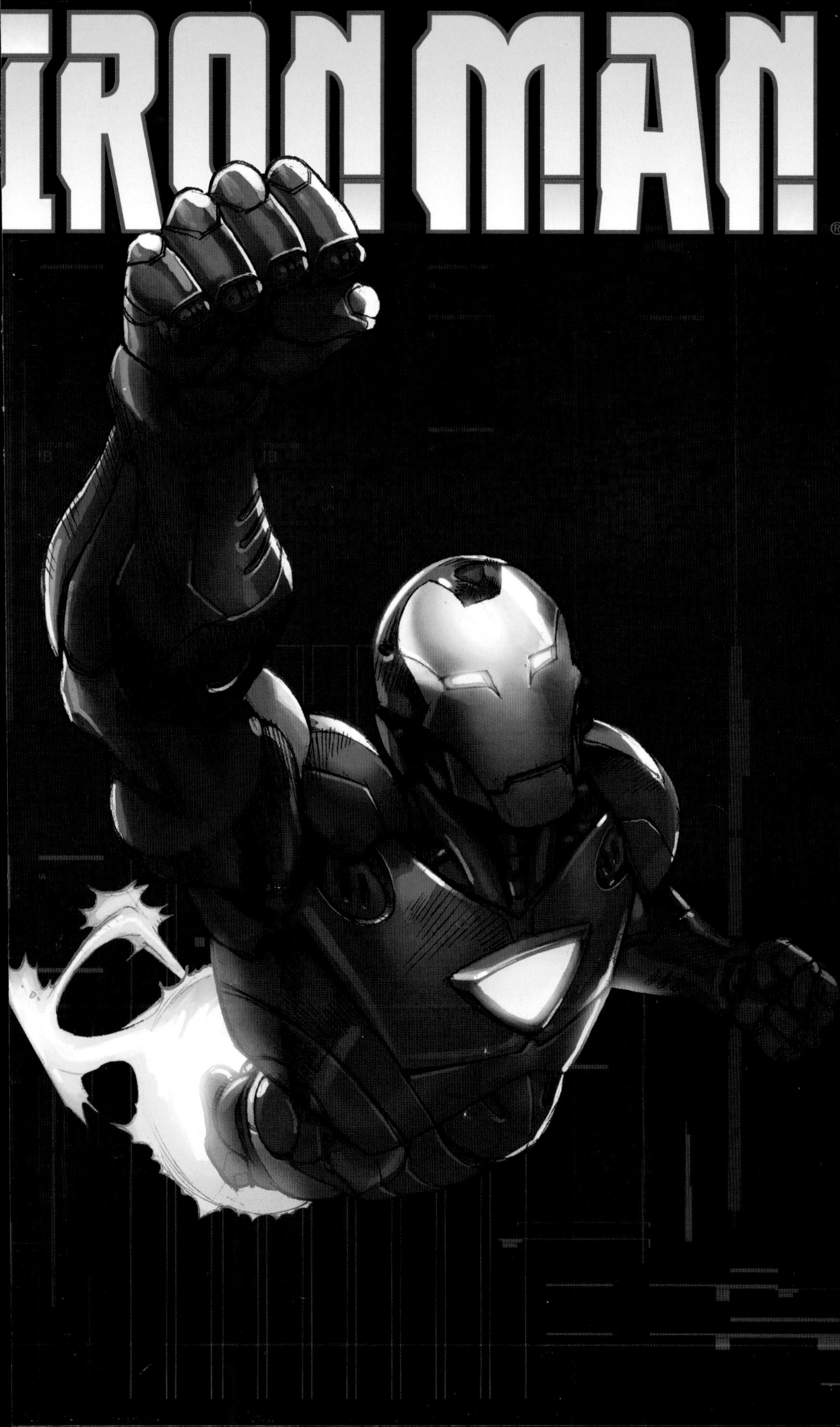
IRON MAN®

VISIT US AT
www.abdopublishing.com

Reinforced library bound edition published in 2011 by Spotlight, a division of the ABDO Group, 8000 West 78th Street, Edina, Minnesota 55439. Spotlight produces high-quality reinforced library bound editions for schools and libraries. Published by agreement with Marvel Characters, Inc.

Printed in the United States of America, Melrose Park, Illinois.
042010
092010
This book contains at least 10% recycled material.

Library of Congress Cataloging-in-Publication Data

Van Lente, Fred.
  Kiber the cruel / story, Fred Van Lente ; art, Scott Koblish.
     p. cm. -- (Iron Man)
  "Marvel."
  ISBN 978-1-59961-772-5
  1. Graphic novels. [1. Graphic novels. 2. Superheroes--Fiction.] I. Koblish, Scott, ill. II. Title.
  PZ7.7.V26Kib 2010
  741.5'973--dc22
                              2009052837

All Spotlight books have reinforced library bindings and
are manufactured in the United States of America.

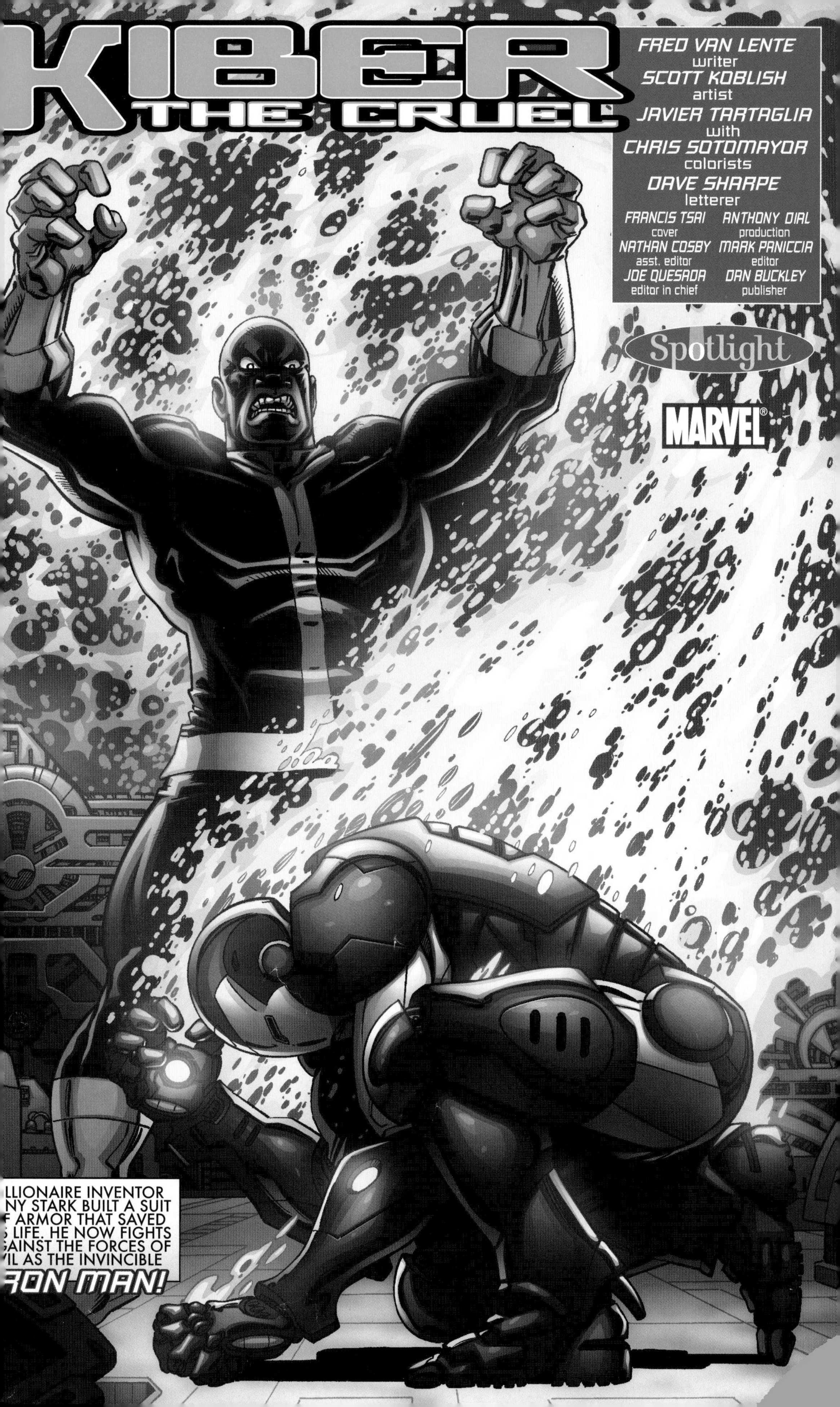

KIBER THE CRUEL
FRED VAN LENTE writer
SCOTT KOBLISH artist
JAVIER TARTAGLIA with CHRIS SOTOMAYOR colorists
DAVE SHARPE letterer
FRANCIS TSAI cover
ANTHONY DIAL production
NATHAN COSBY asst. editor
MARK PANICCIA editor
JOE QUESADA editor in chief
DAN BUCKLEY publisher
Spotlight
MARVEL
LLIONAIRE INVENTOR NY STARK BUILT A SUIT F ARMOR THAT SAVED S LIFE. HE NOW FIGHTS GAINST THE FORCES OF VIL AS THE INVINCIBLE
RON MAN!

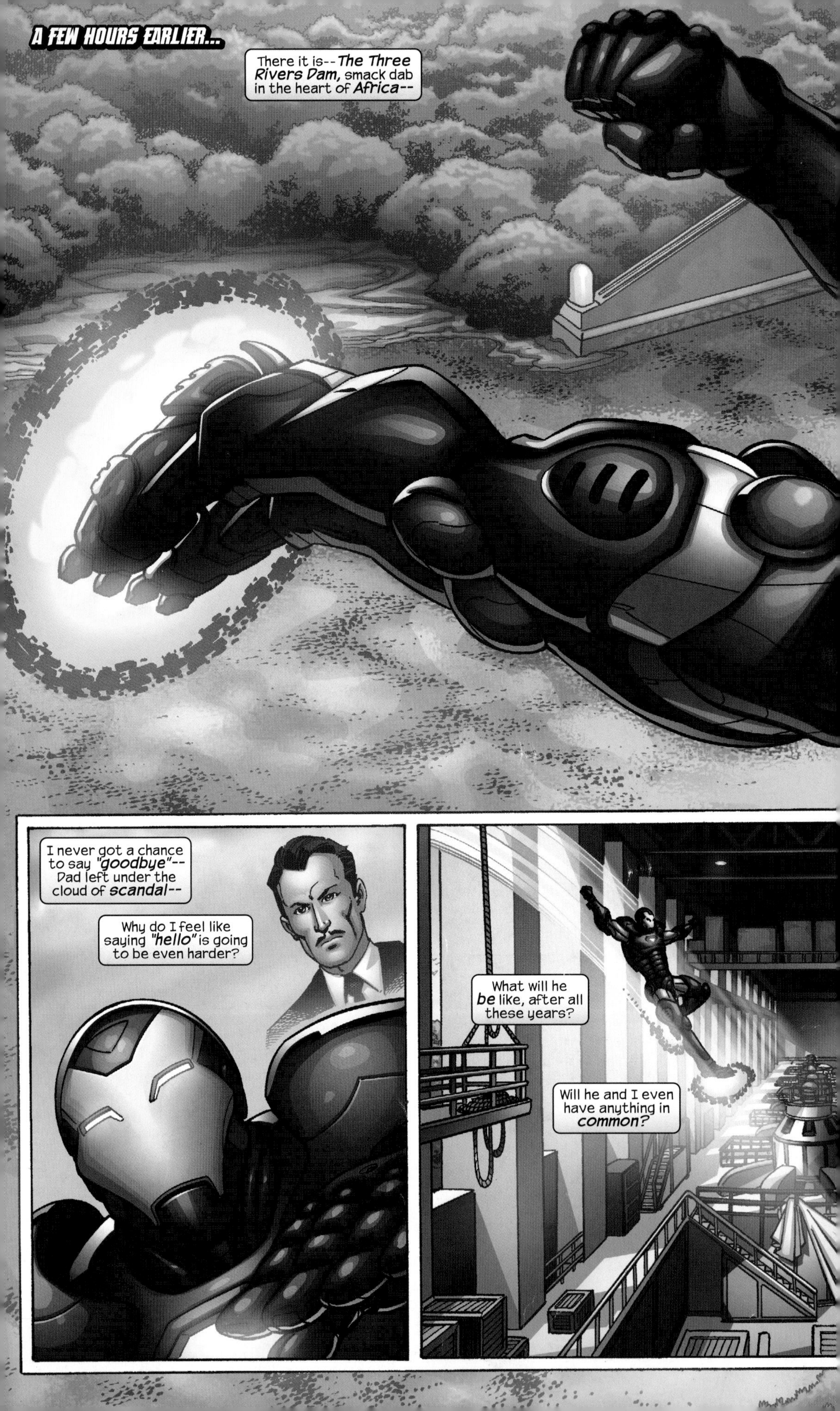
A FEW HOURS EARLIER...
There it is--The Three Rivers Dam, smack dab in the heart of Africa--
I never got a chance to say "goodbye"-- Dad left under the cloud of scandal--
Why do I feel like saying "hello" is going to be even harder?
What will he be like, after all these years?
Will he and I even have anything in common?

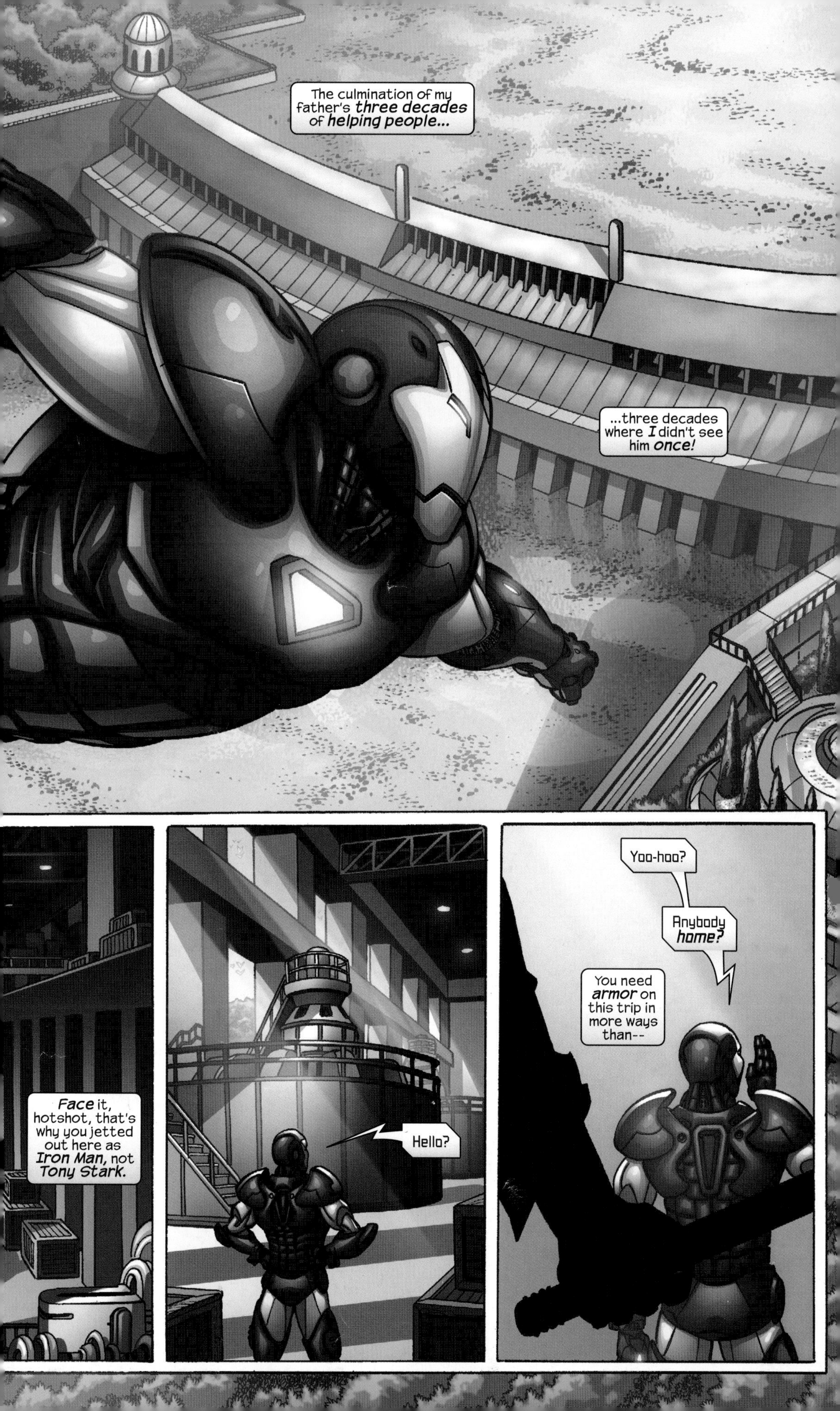
The culmination of my father's *three decades* of *helping people...*
...three decades where *I* didn't see him *once!*
Face it, hotshot, that's why you jetted out here as *Iron Man,* not *Tony Stark.*
Hello?
Yoo-hoo?
Anybody *home?*
You need *armor* on this trip in more ways than--

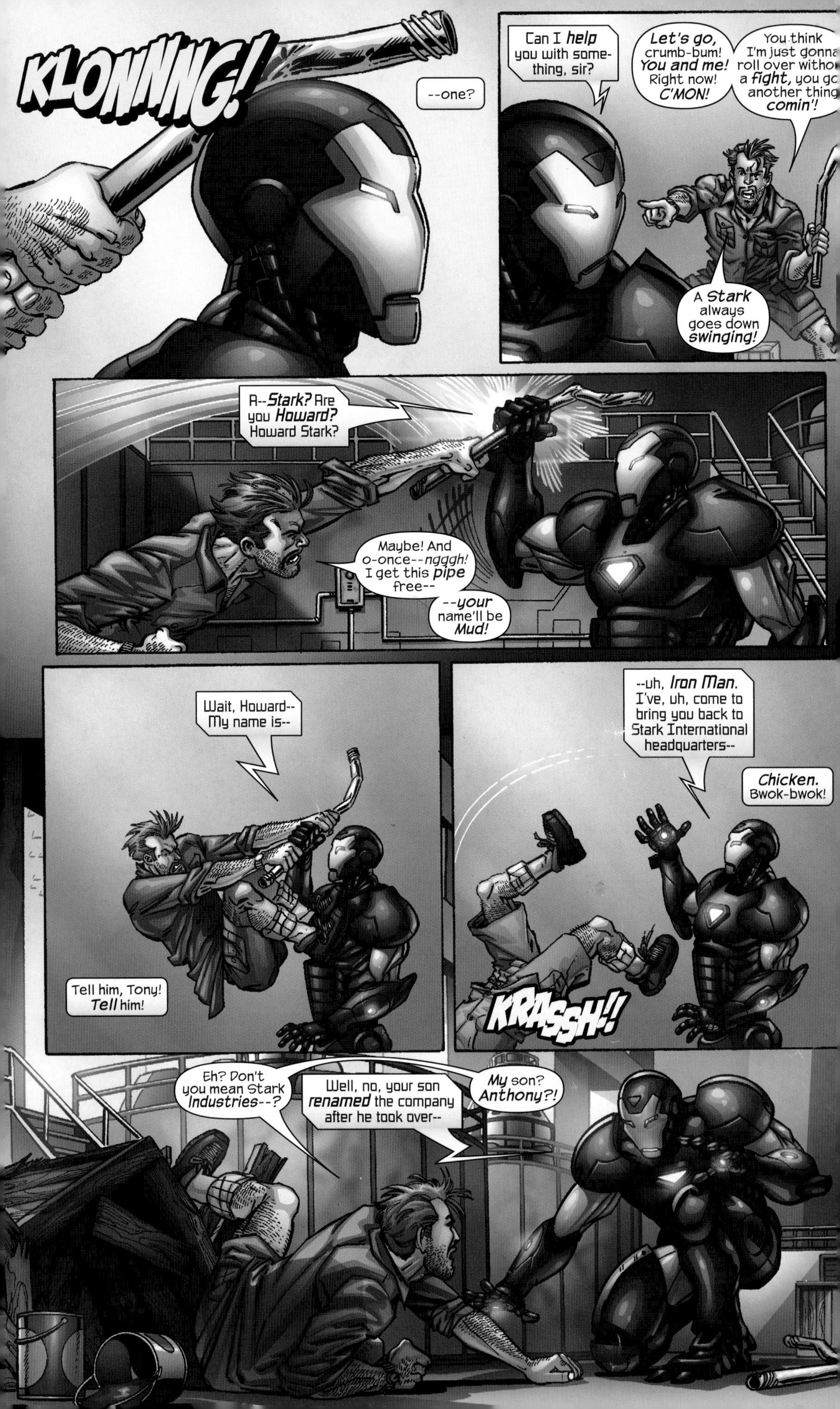
KLONNNG!
--one?
Can I help you with something, sir?
Let's go, crumb-bum! You and me! Right now! C'MON!
You think I'm just gonna roll over witho a fight, you go another thing comin'!
A Stark always goes down swinging!
A--Stark? Are you Howard? Howard Stark?
Maybe! And o-once--ngggh! I get this pipe free--
--your name'll be Mud!
Wait, Howard-- My name is--
Tell him, Tony! Tell him!
--uh, Iron Man. I've, uh, come to bring you back to Stark International headquarters--
Chicken. Bwok-bwok!
KRASSH!!
Eh? Don't you mean Stark Industries--?
Well, no, your son renamed the company after he took over--
My son? Anthony?!

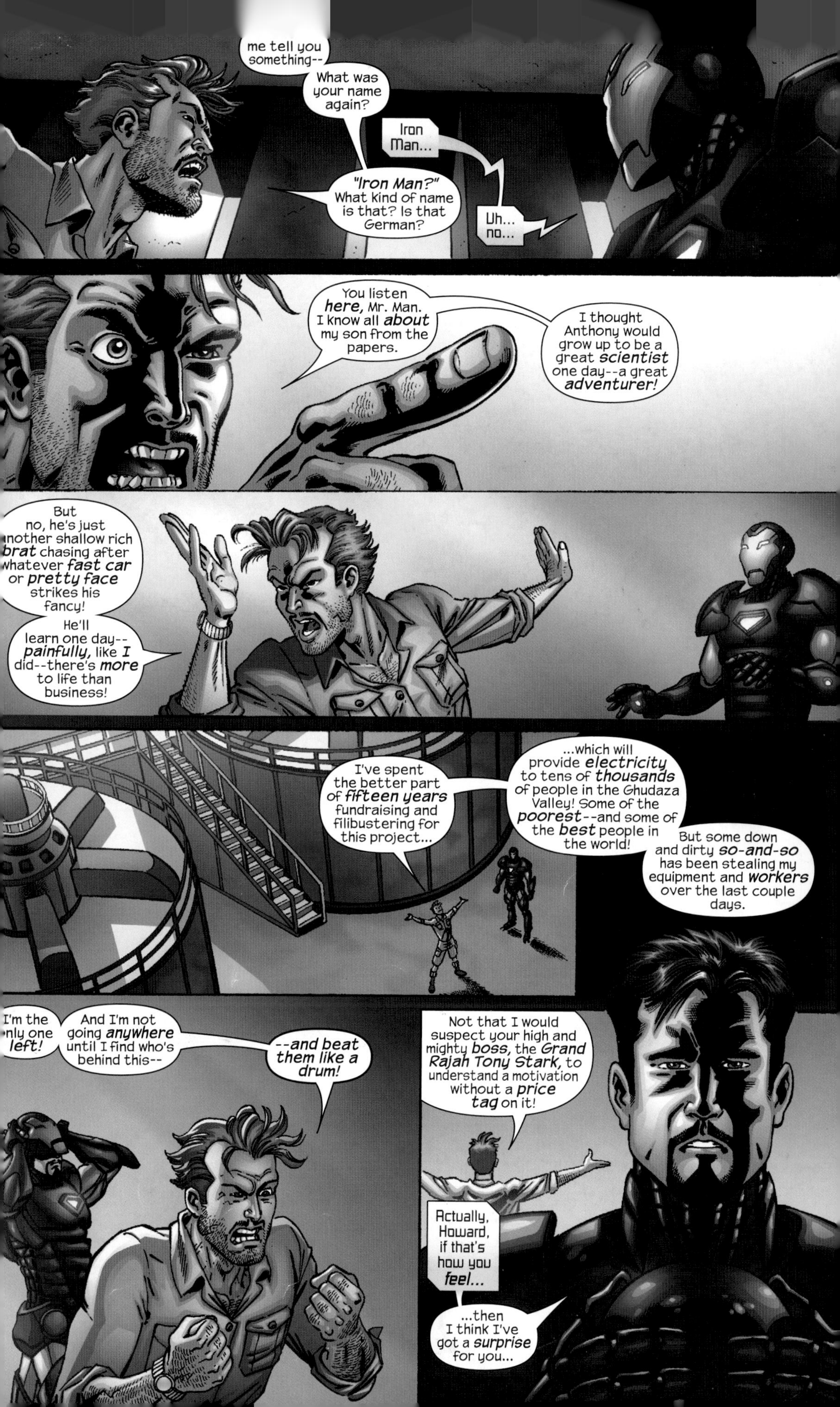
me tell you something--
What was your name again?
Iron Man...
"Iron Man?" What kind of name is that? Is that German?
Uh... no...
You listen here, Mr. Man. I know all about my son from the papers.
I thought Anthony would grow up to be a great scientist one day--a great adventurer!
But no, he's just another shallow rich brat chasing after whatever fast car or pretty face strikes his fancy!
He'll learn one day--painfully, like I did--there's more to life than business!
I've spent the better part of fifteen years fundraising and filibustering for this project...
...which will provide electricity to tens of thousands of people in the Ghudaza Valley! Some of the poorest--and some of the best people in the world!
But some down and dirty so-and-so has been stealing my equipment and workers over the last couple days.
I'm the only one left!
And I'm not going anywhere until I find who's behind this--
--and beat them like a drum!
Not that I would suspect your high and mighty boss, the Grand Rajah Tony Stark, to understand a motivation without a price tag on it!
Actually, Howard, if that's how you feel...
...then I think I've got a surprise for you...

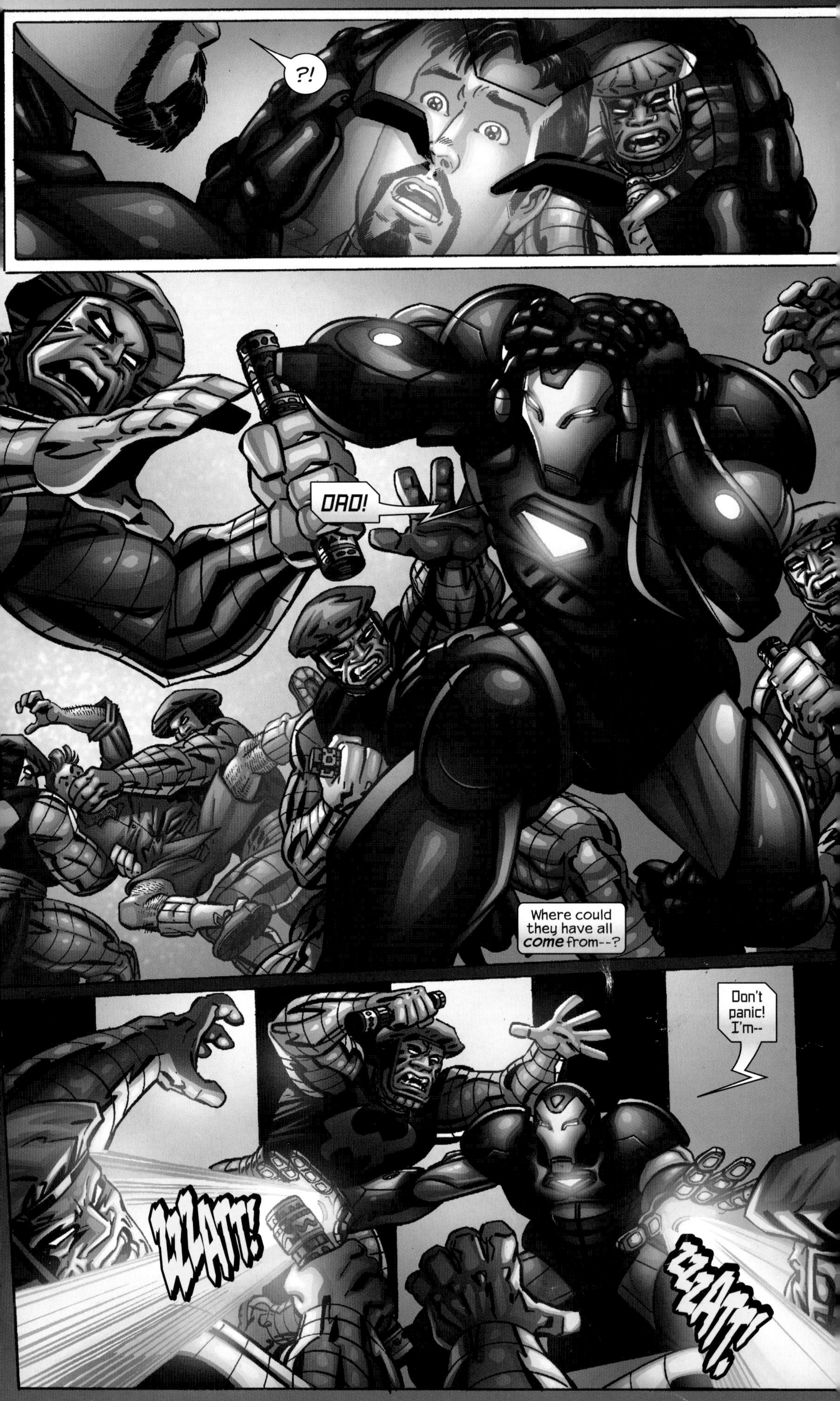
?!
DAD!
Where could they have all come from--?
Don't panic! I'm--
ZZZAT!
ZZAT!

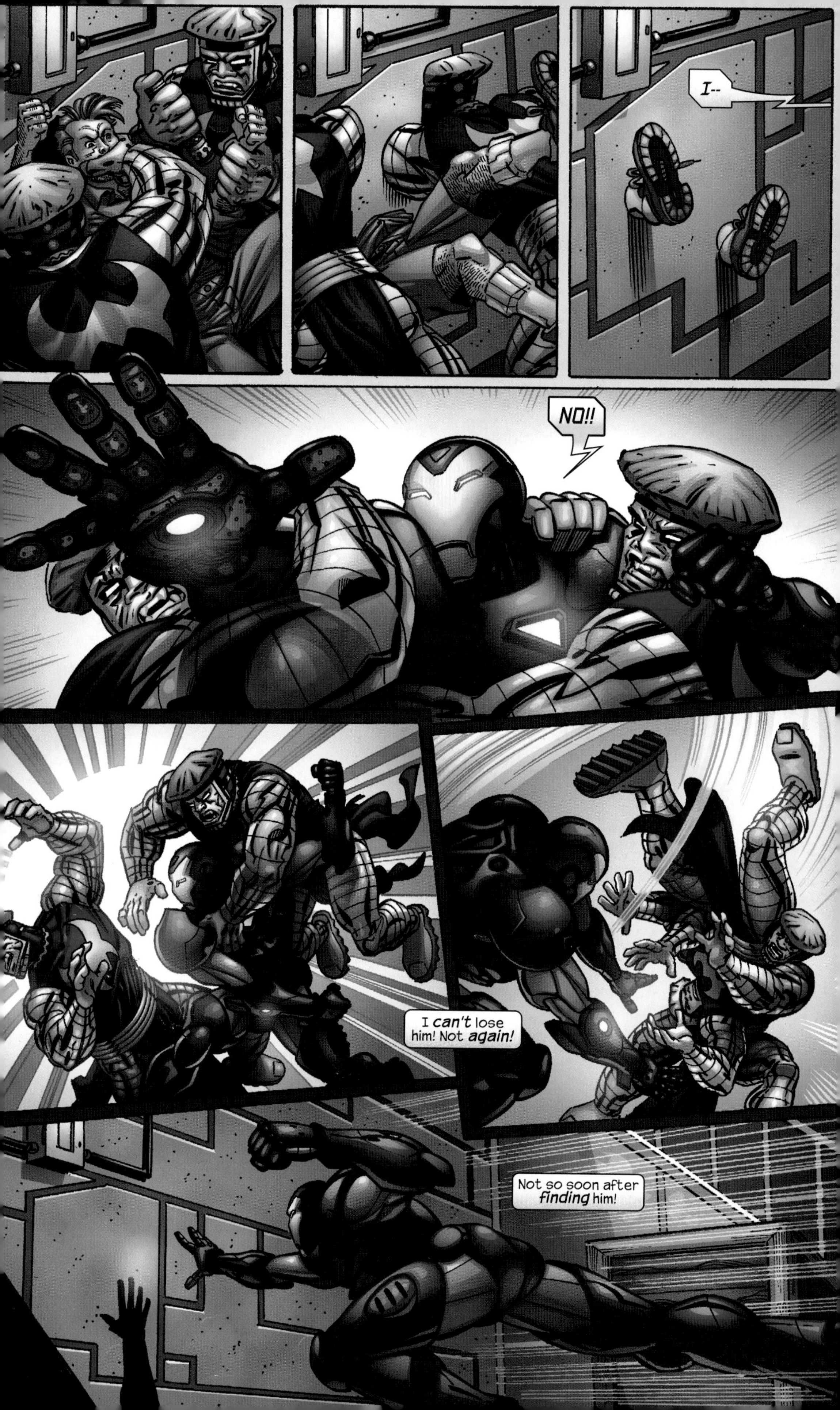

I--
NO!!
I *can't* lose him! Not *again!*
Not so soon after *finding* him!

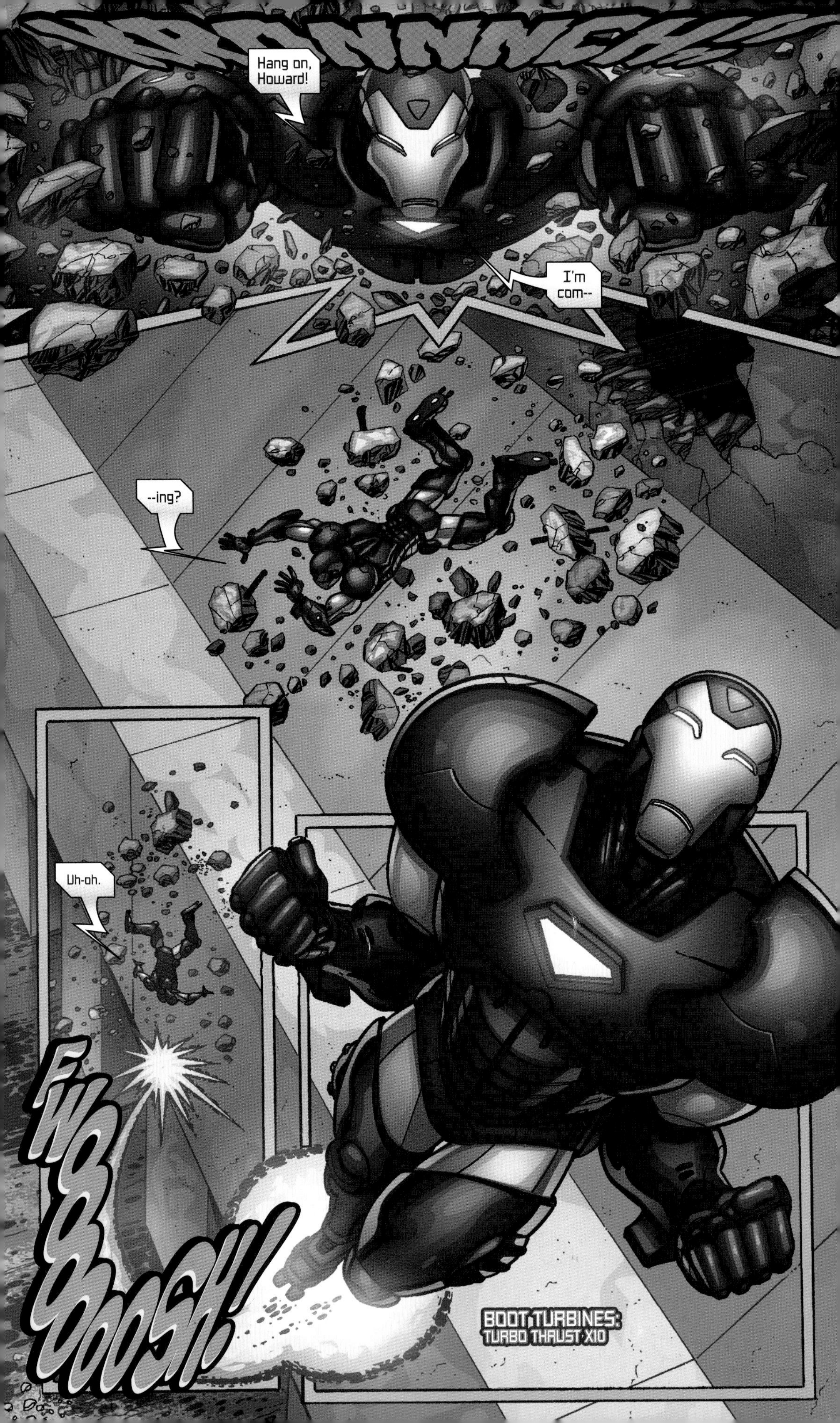
Hang on, Howard!
I'm com--
--ing?
Uh-oh.
BOOT TURBINES:
TURBO THRUST X10

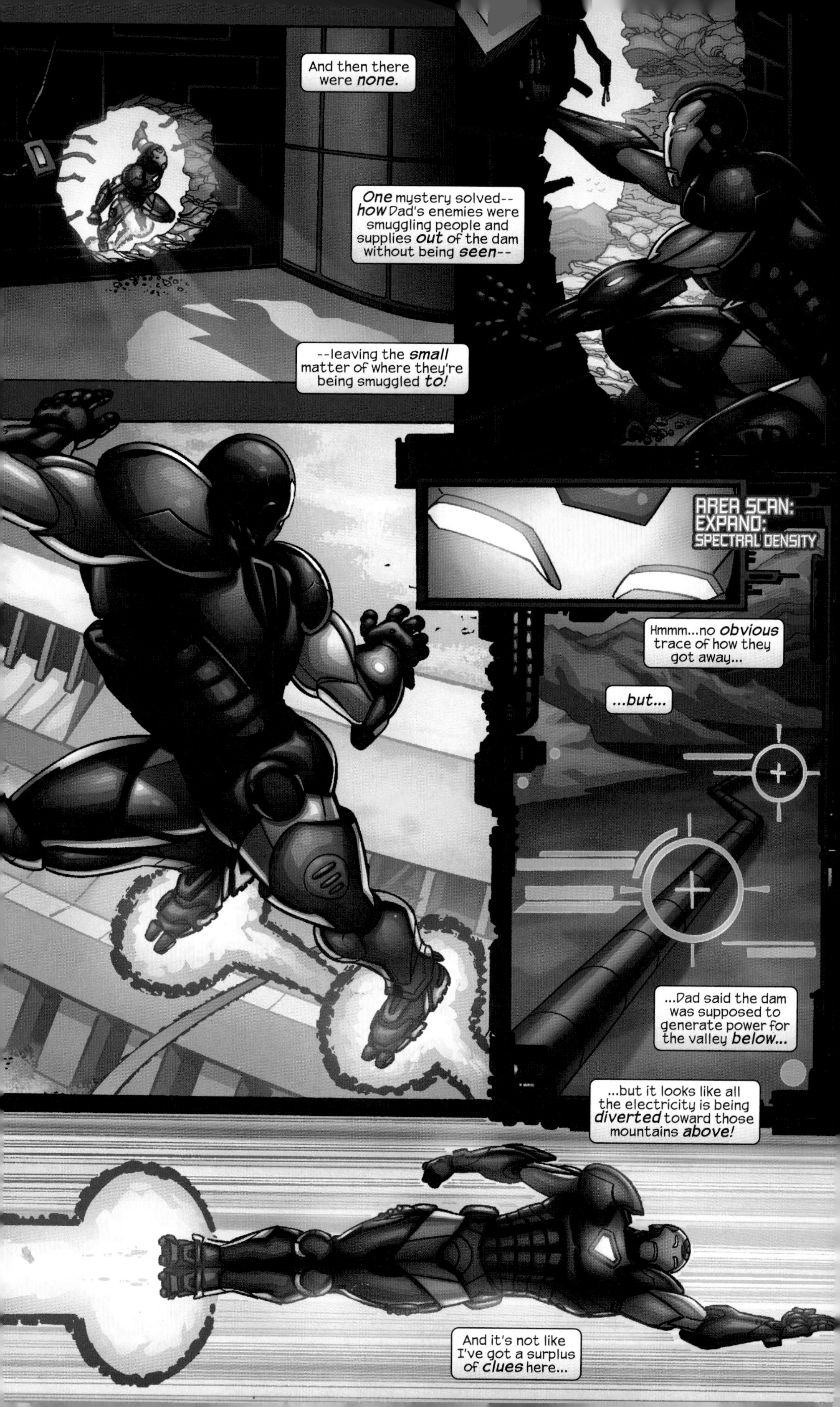
And then there were *none.*
One mystery solved-- *how* Dad's enemies were smuggling people and supplies *out* of the dam without being *seen*--
--leaving the *small* matter of where they're being smuggled *to!*
AREA SCAN:
EXPAND:
SPECTRAL DENSITY
Hmmm...no *obvious* trace of how they got away...
...but...
...Dad said the dam was supposed to generate power for the valley *below...*
...but it looks like all the electricity is being *diverted* toward those mountains *above!*
And it's not like I've got a surplus of *clues* here...

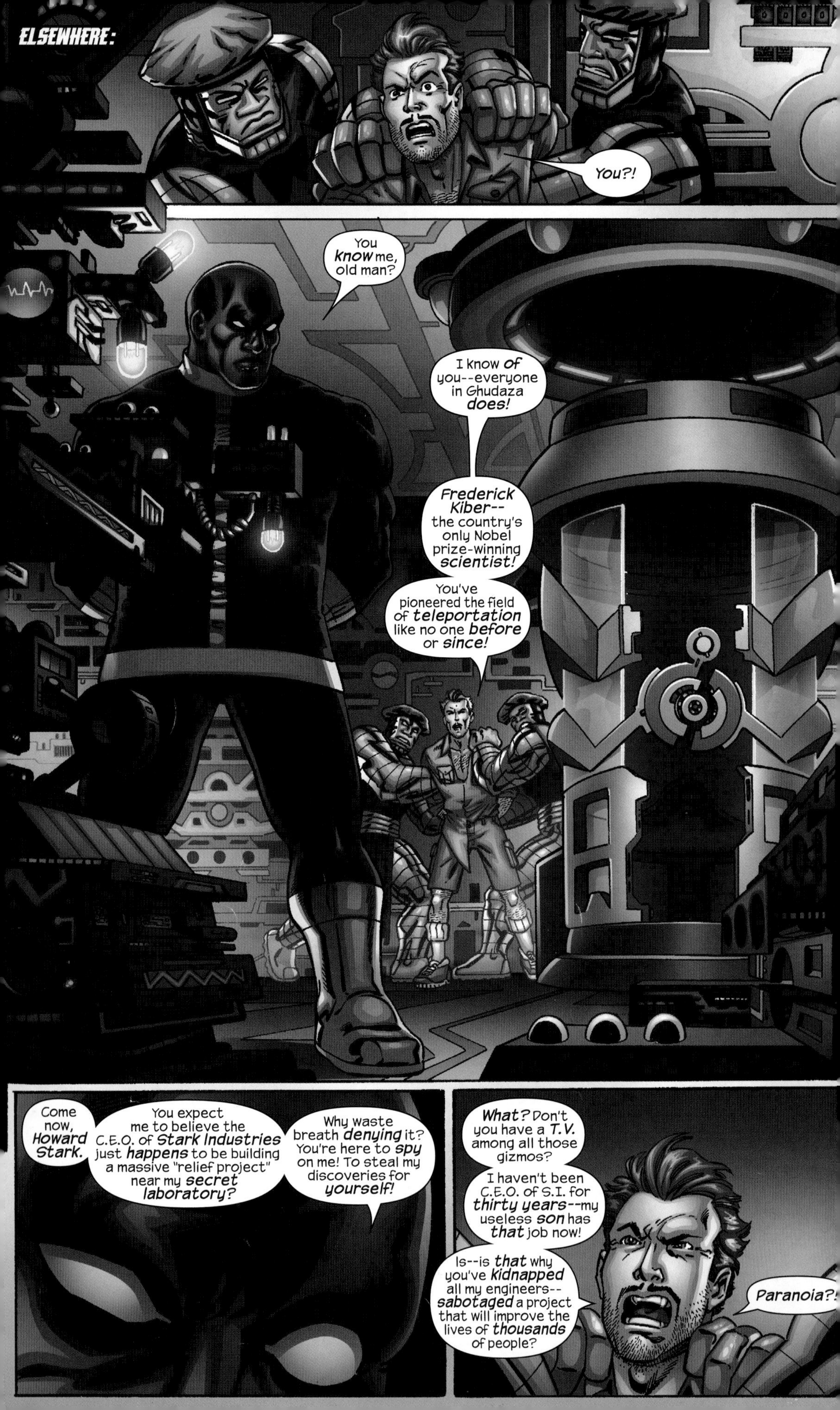
ELSEWHERE:
You?!
You know me, old man?
I know of you--everyone in Ghudaza does!
Frederick Kiber-- the country's only Nobel prize-winning scientist!
You've pioneered the field of teleportation like no one before or since!
Come now, Howard Stark.
You expect me to believe the C.E.O. of Stark Industries just happens to be building a massive "relief project" near my secret laboratory?
Why waste breath denying it? You're here to spy on me! To steal my discoveries for yourself!
What? Don't you have a T.V. among all those gizmos?
I haven't been C.E.O. of S.I. for thirty years--my useless son has that job now!
Is--is that why you've kidnapped all my engineers--sabotaged a project that will improve the lives of thousands of people?
Paranoia?!

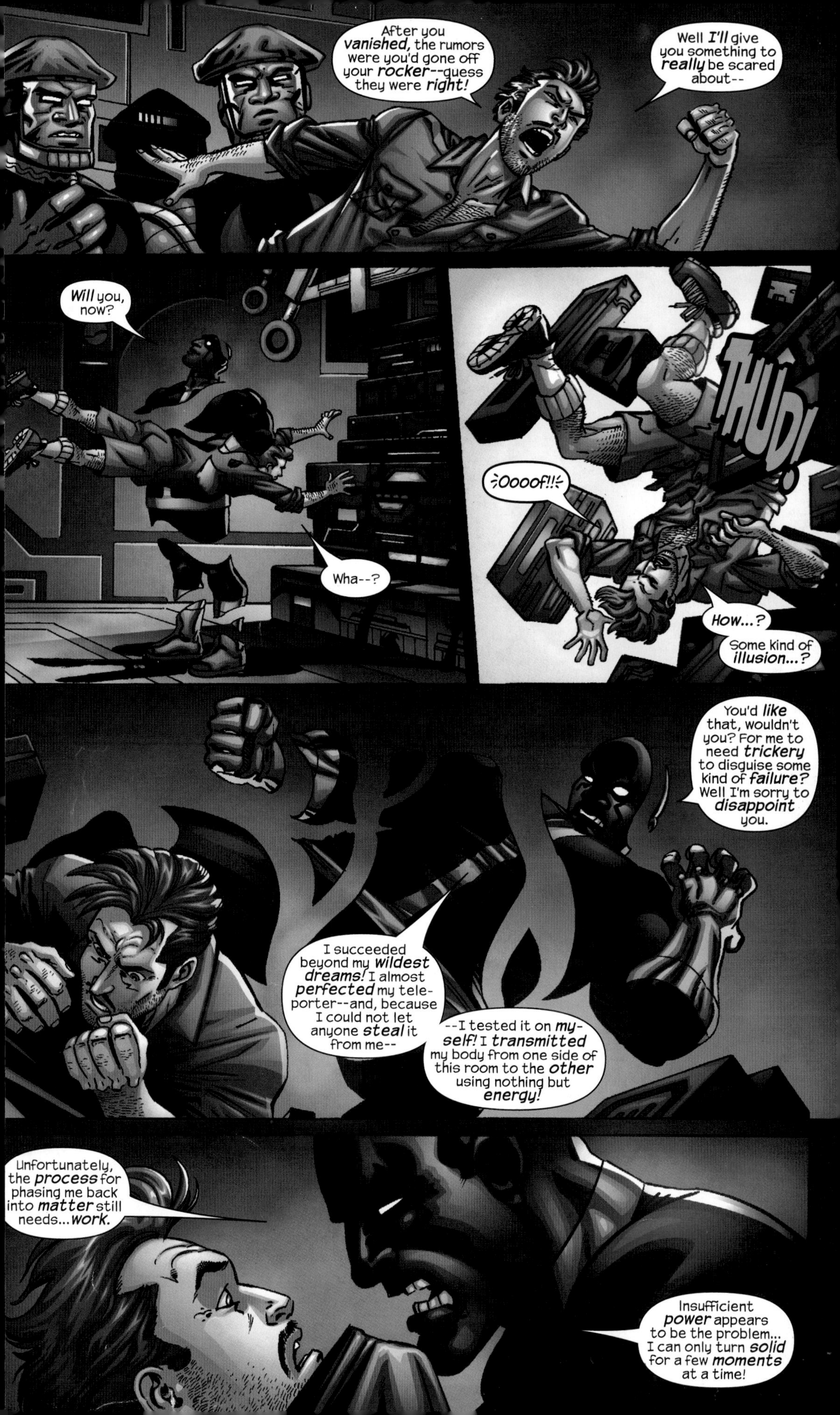
After you vanished, the rumors were you'd gone off your rocker--guess they were right!
Well I'll give you something to really be scared about--
Will you, now?
Wha--?
THUD!
Oooof!!
How...?
Some kind of illusion...?
You'd like that, wouldn't you? For me to need trickery to disguise some kind of failure? Well I'm sorry to disappoint you.
I succeeded beyond my wildest dreams! I almost perfected my teleporter--and, because I could not let anyone steal it from me--
--I tested it on myself! I transmitted my body from one side of this room to the other using nothing but energy!
Unfortunately, the process for phasing me back into matter still needs...work.
Insufficient power appears to be the problem... I can only turn solid for a few moments at a time!

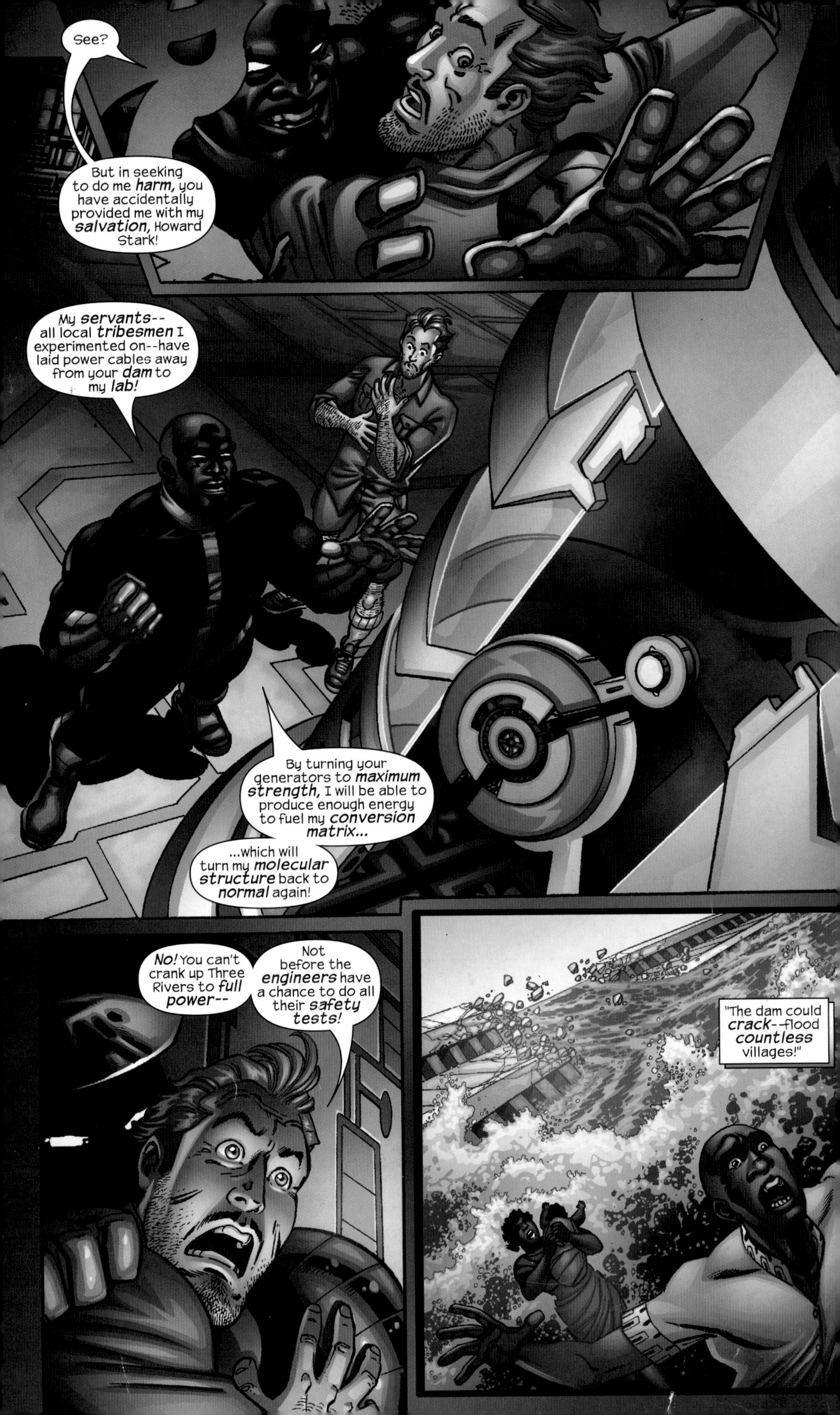
See?
But in seeking to do me *harm*, you have accidentally provided me with my *salvation*, Howard Stark!
My *servants*-- all local *tribesmen* I experimented on--have laid power cables away from your *dam* to my *lab!*
By turning your generators to *maximum strength*, I will be able to produce enough energy to fuel my *conversion matrix...*
...which will turn my *molecular structure* back to *normal* again!
No! You can't crank up Three Rivers to *full power--*
Not before the *engineers* have a chance to do all their *safety tests!*
"The dam could *crack*--flood *countless* villages!"

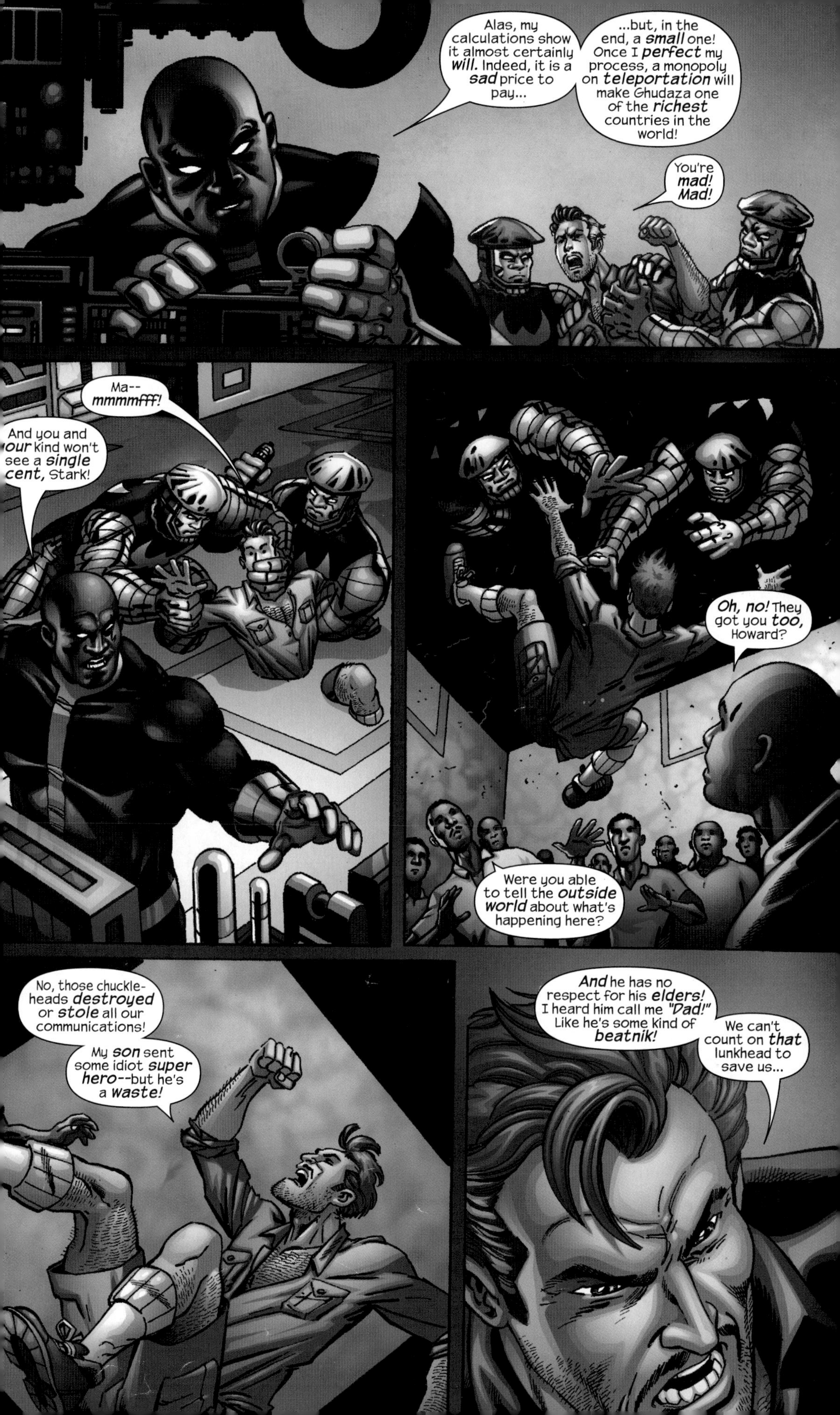
Alas, my calculations show it almost certainly will. Indeed, it is a sad price to pay...
...but, in the end, a small one! Once I perfect my process, a monopoly on teleportation will make Ghudaza one of the richest countries in the world!
You're mad! Mad!
Ma-- mmmmfff!
And you and our kind won't see a single cent, Stark!
Oh, no! They got you too, Howard?
Were you able to tell the outside world about what's happening here?
No, those chuckle-heads destroyed or stole all our communications!
My son sent some idiot super hero--but he's a waste!
And he has no respect for his elders! I heard him call me "Dad!" Like he's some kind of beatnik!
We can't count on that lunkhead to save us...

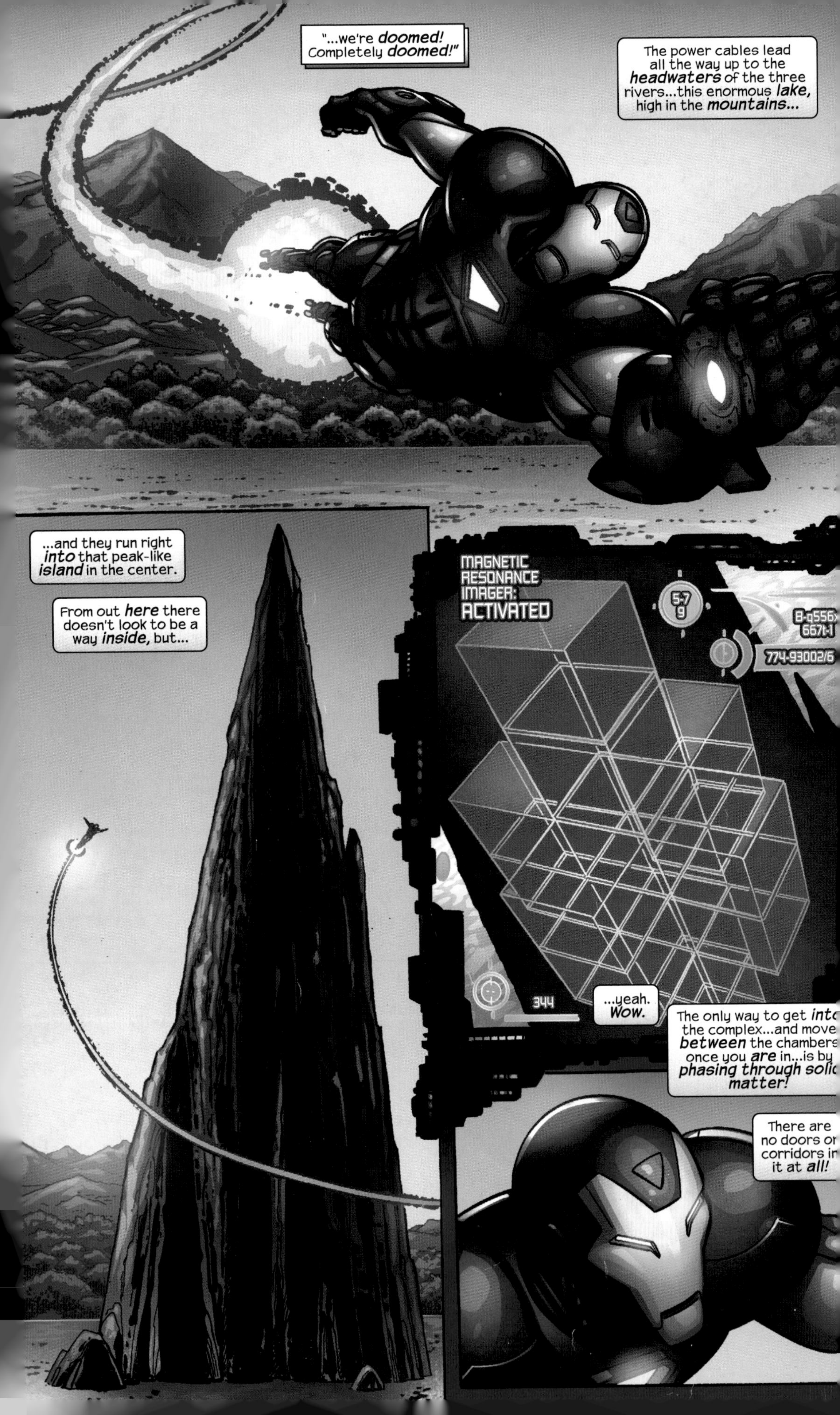
"...we're doomed! Completely doomed!"
The power cables lead all the way up to the headwaters of the three rivers...this enormous lake, high in the mountains...
...and they run right into that peak-like island in the center.
From out here there doesn't look to be a way inside, but...
MAGNETIC RESONANCE IMAGER: ACTIVATED
5-7 9
774-93002/6
344
...yeah. Wow.
The only way to get into the complex...and move between the chambers once you are in...is by phasing through solid matter!
There are no doors or corridors in it at all!

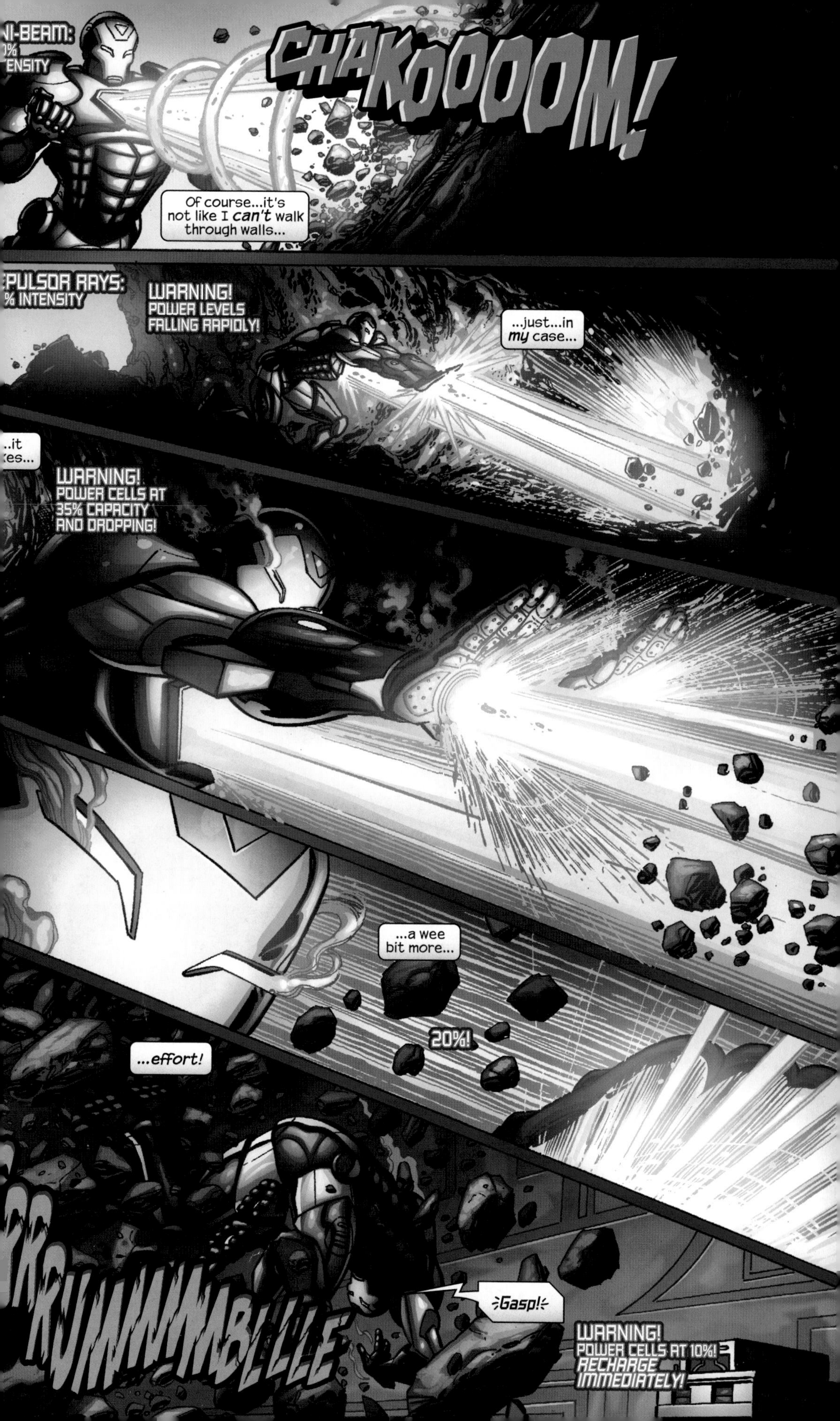

NI-BEAM:
0%
ENSITY
CHAKOOOOM!
Of course...it's not like I can't walk through walls...
EPULSOR RAYS:
% INTENSITY
WARNING! POWER LEVELS FALLING RAPIDLY!
...just...in my case...
...it
es...
WARNING! POWER CELLS AT 35% CAPACITY AND DROPPING!
...a wee bit more...
20%!
...effort!
KRUMMMMBLLLE
Gasp!
WARNING! POWER CELLS AT 10%! RECHARGE IMMEDIATELY!

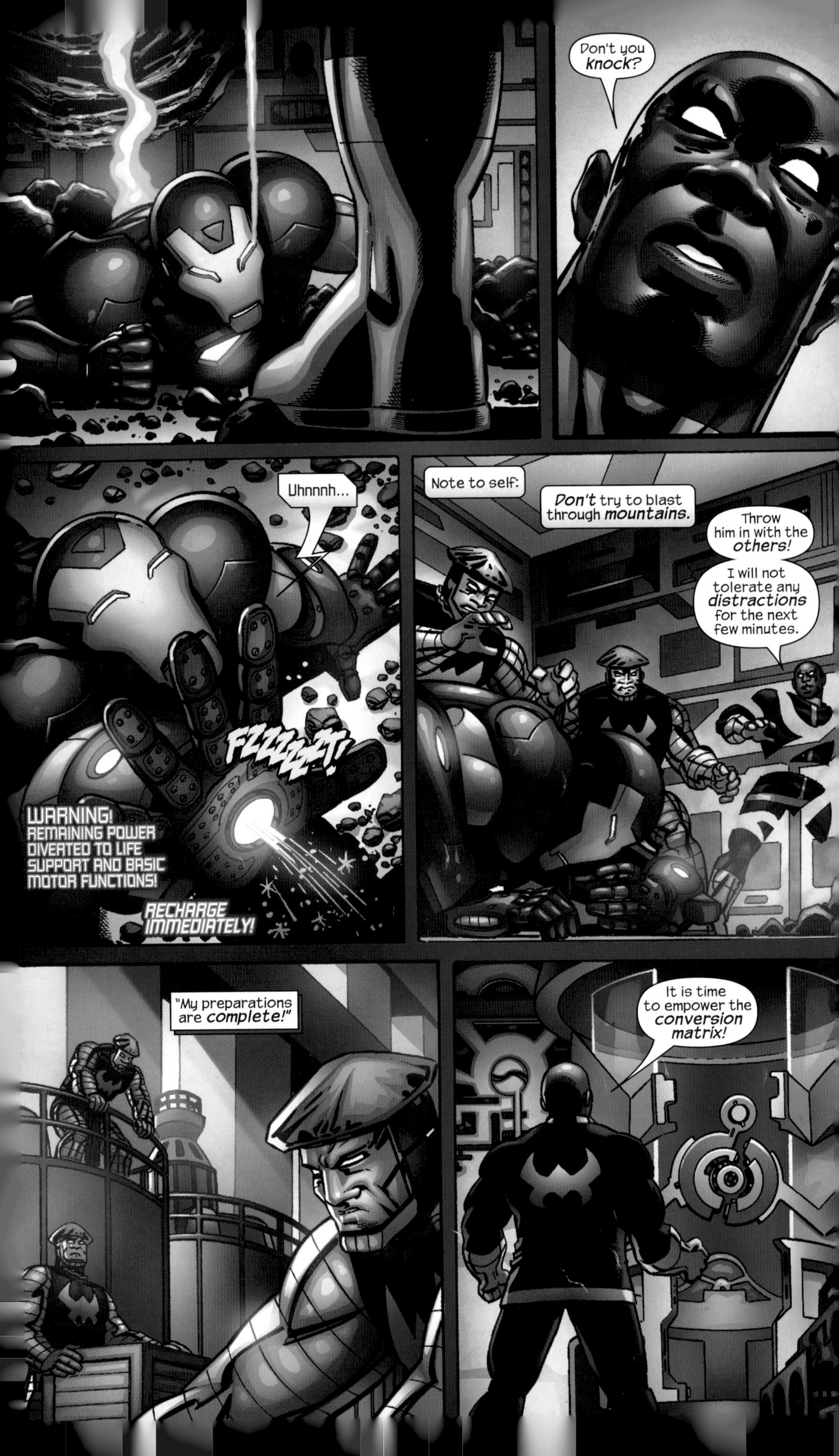

Don't you knock?
Uhnnnh...
FZZZZZT!
WARNING! REMAINING POWER DIVERTED TO LIFE SUPPORT AND BASIC MOTOR FUNCTIONS!
RECHARGE IMMEDIATELY!
Note to self:
Don't try to blast through mountains.
Throw him in with the others!
I will not tolerate any distractions for the next few minutes.
"My preparations are complete!"
It is time to empower the conversion matrix!

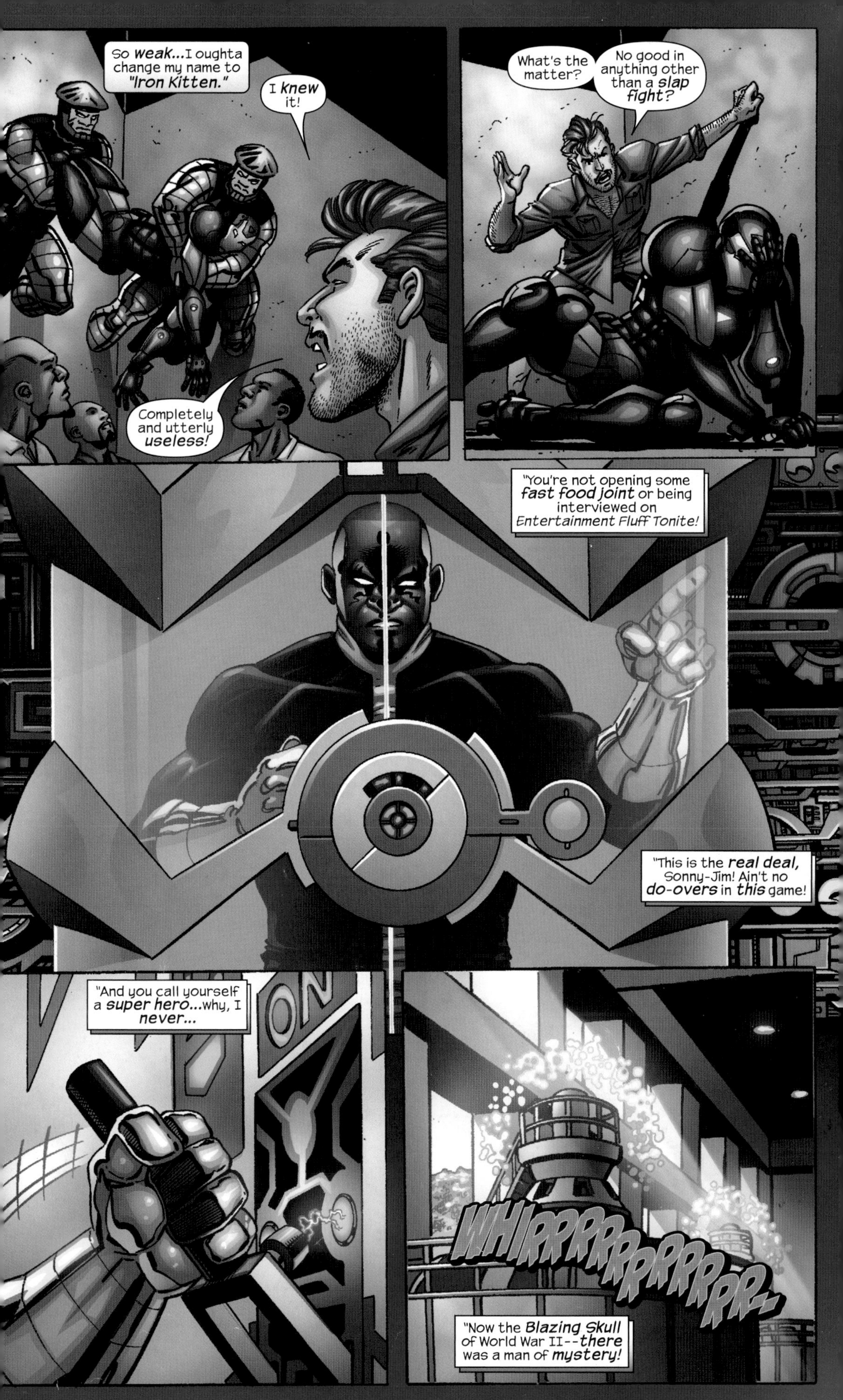
So weak...I oughta change my name to "Iron Kitten."
I knew it!
Completely and utterly useless!
What's the matter?
No good in anything other than a slap fight?
"You're not opening some fast food joint or being interviewed on Entertainment Fluff Tonite!
"This is the real deal, Sonny-Jim! Ain't no do-overs in this game!
"And you call yourself a super hero...why, I never...
WHIRRRRRRRRRRRR
"Now the Blazing Skull of World War II--there was a man of mystery!

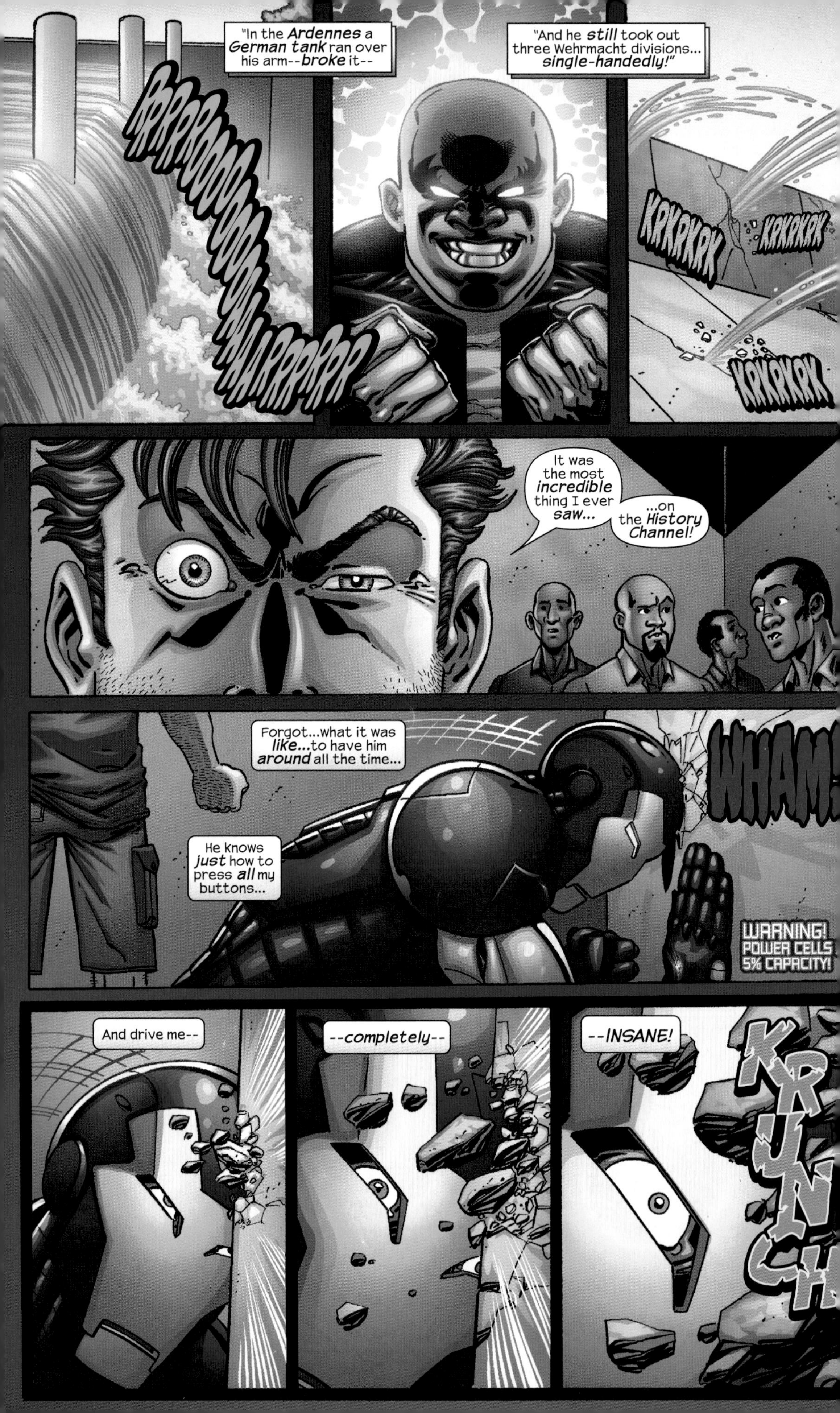

"In the Ardennes a German tank ran over his arm--broke it--
RRRROOOOOOOOOAAARRRRRR
"And he still took out three Wehrmacht divisions... single-handedly!"
KRKRKRK
KRKRKRK
KRKRKRK
It was the most incredible thing I ever saw...
...on the History Channel!
Forgot...what it was like...to have him around all the time...
WHAM!
He knows just how to press all my buttons...
WARNING! POWER CELLS 5% CAPACITY!
And drive me--
--completely--
--INSANE!
KRUNCH

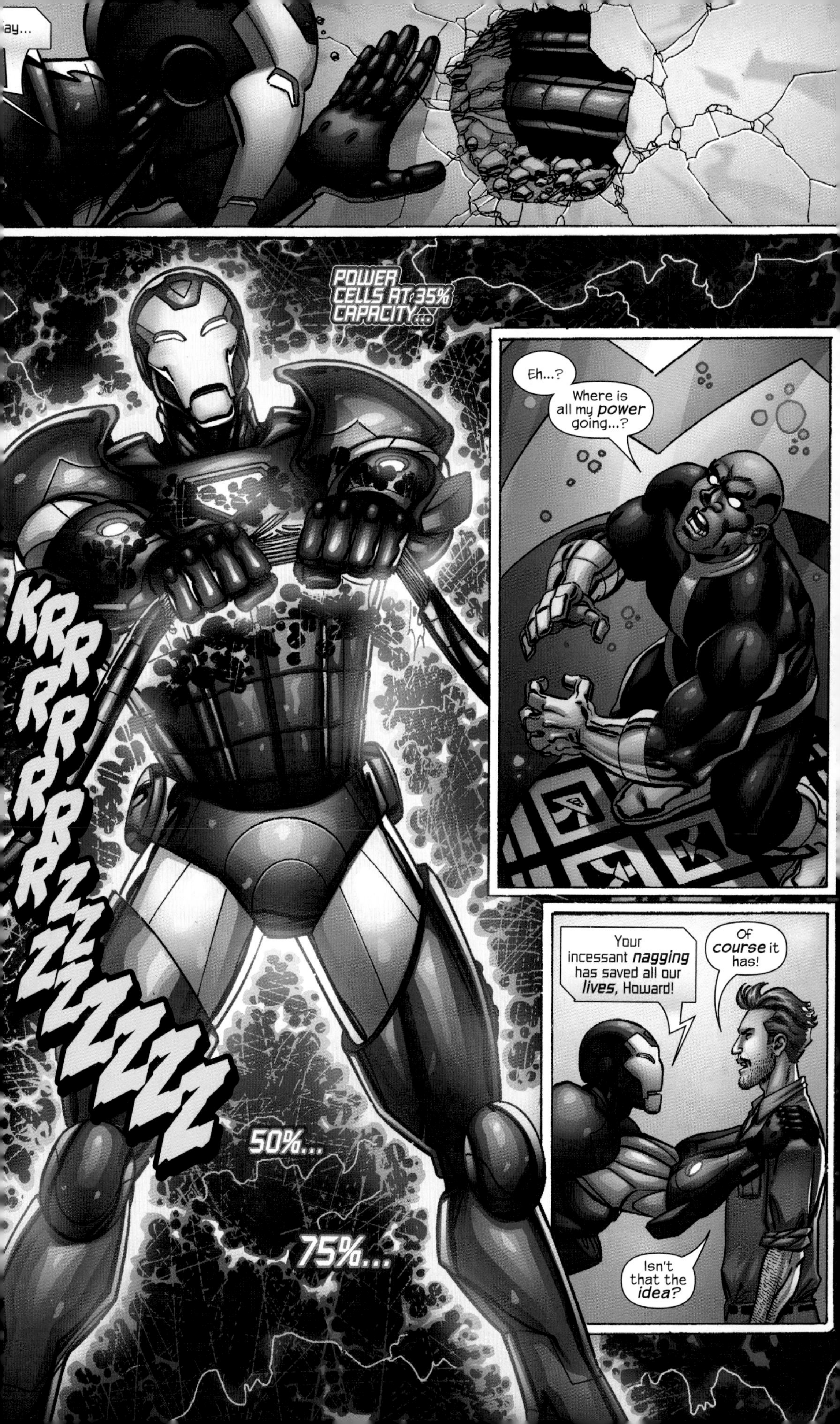

ay...
POWER CELLS AT 35% CAPACITY...
KRRRRRRRZZZZZZZZ
50%...
75%...
Eh...?
Where is all my *power* going...?
Your incessant *nagging* has saved all our *lives*, Howard!
Of *course* it has!
Isn't that the *idea*?

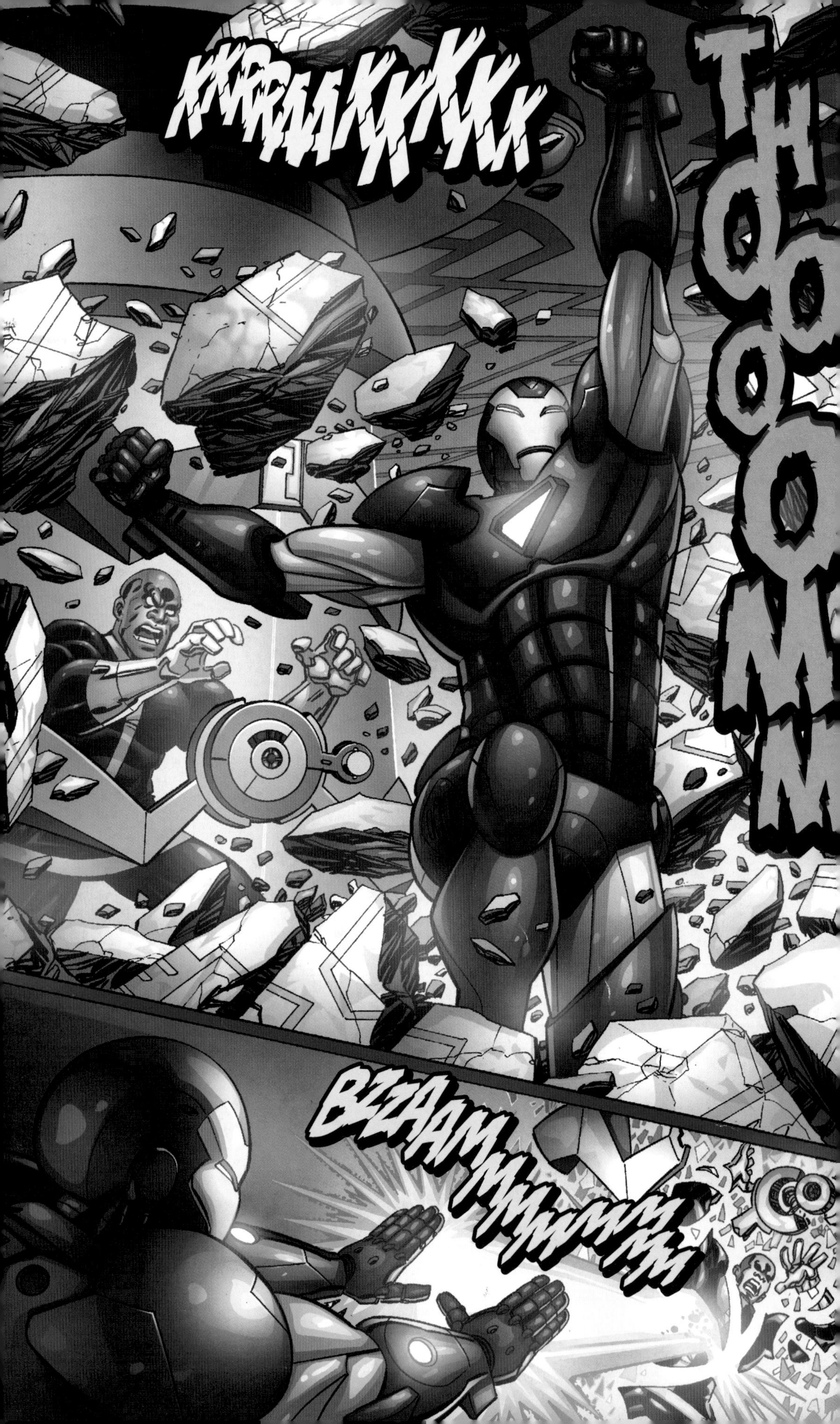
KKRAAKKKKK
THOOOMM
BZZAAMMMMMM

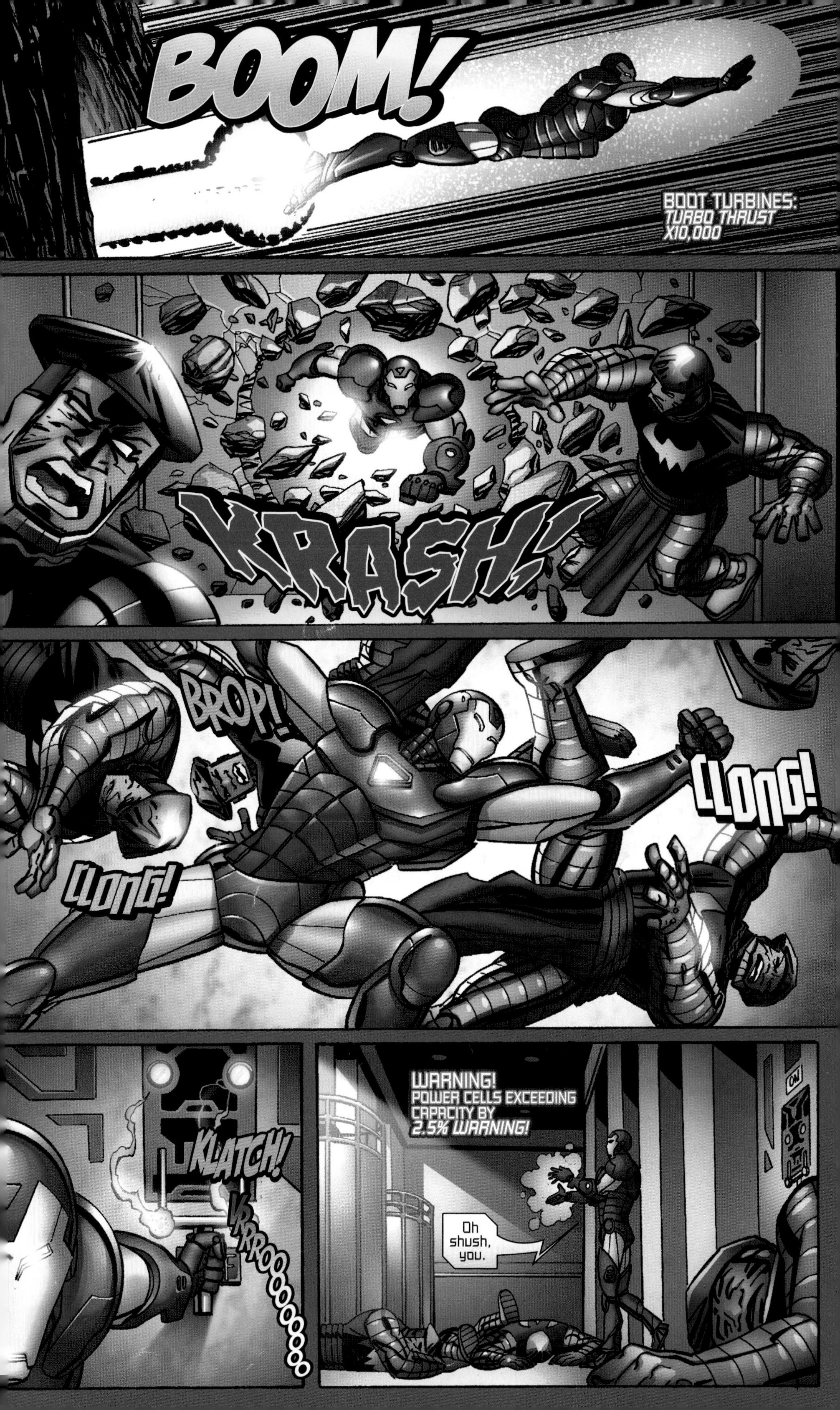

BOOM!
BOOT TURBINES:
TURBO THRUST
X10,000
KRASH!
BROP!
CLONG!
CLONG!
KLATCH!
VRRROOOOOOOO
WARNING!
POWER CELLS EXCEEDING
CAPACITY BY
2.5% WARNING!
Oh shush, you.

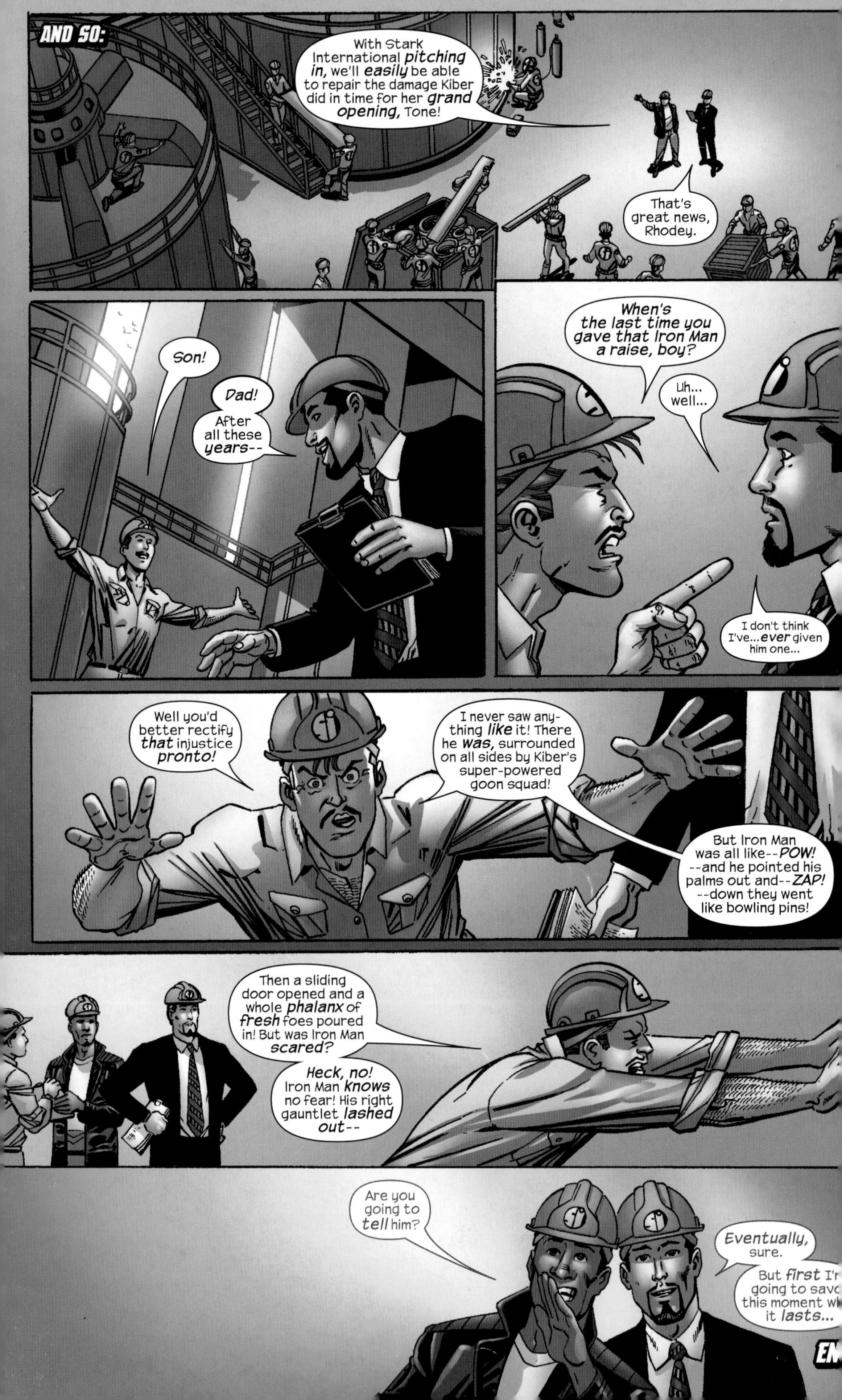
AND SO:
With Stark International pitching in, we'll easily be able to repair the damage Kiber did in time for her grand opening, Tone!
That's great news, Rhodey.
Son!
Dad!
After all these years--
When's the last time you gave that Iron Man a raise, boy?
Uh... well...
I don't think I've...ever given him one...
Well you'd better rectify that injustice pronto!
I never saw any-thing like it! There he was, surrounded on all sides by Kiber's super-powered goon squad!
But Iron Man was all like--POW! --and he pointed his palms out and--ZAP! --down they went like bowling pins!
Then a sliding door opened and a whole phalanx of fresh foes poured in! But was Iron Man scared?
Heck, no! Iron Man knows no fear! His right gauntlet lashed out--
Are you going to tell him?
Eventually, sure.